Gerda,
May the Story
Thabo, encourage you, of
God's love.
Love,
Laurie
+xoo

MW01041820

Thabo's

Village

Written and Illustrated by

Laurie L. Ferris

Laurie L. Ferris

Books by Laurie L. Ferris

Lessons Along The Way

Soul Piercing

Consider His Heart

Thabo's Village

Copyright © 2018 by Laurie L. Ferris

Scripture is from the International Children's Bible

Dedication

Philip Thabo Mangena, you, my brother, have inspired me through the years. Thank you for the many prayers at prayer stall, conversations walking up the hills of Modjadji and the laughter.

This book is a love letter from the Lord to His people, and my gift of appreciation to you for your faithfulness to Jesus Christ. I love and miss you, Thabo, my brother. Keep shining the light of Jesus in the villages God sends you to. You are making an imprint on your side of the globe.

Glossary and Pronunciation Key

Thabo: tah′•bo; person's name; means to rejoice.

Jesu: Jay′•su; Jesus

Wa fisha: wa•fee′•sah; it's hot

Sotho: sue′•too; tribal name of people

Meetse: mate′•see; water

Kraal: crawl; family dwelling

Sopo: so′•po; soup

Thobela le kae: toe•bay′•la lee•guy′; greeting

Re gona le kae: ree•on′•a lee•guy′; I am well

Tate: taa′•tee; father

Dijo: dee′•joe; food

Eish: eesh; wow or amazed

Moruti: mo•roo′•tee; pastor

Melie: me′•lee; corn

Gabotsi: ha•boot′•see; go well

Robala gabotsi: row•bay′•la ha•boot′•see; have a good rest, or sleep, go well.

"O atišitše setšhaba, Morena; o se thabišitše kudu. Ba thabile pele ga gago, ba swana le batho ba ba thabetšego go buna, goba go arolelana dithebola" Isaiah 9:2

Northern Pedi Bible

"Now those people live in darkness. But they will see a great light. They live in a place that is very dark. But a light will shine on them." Isaiah 9:2

International Children's Bible

"Joshua, my son, we must walk up the mountain and see all that is going on in Thabo's village. I've been hearing from the villagers such wonderful stories about the love of *Jesu*."

"Oh, Father, do you think when we get to Thabo's village there will be an elephant?"

"No, Joshua, elephants no longer roam freely and won't be in Thabo's village."

"Will I see a lion and hear him roar?"

"No, Joshua. Lions are fierce. You wouldn't want to see one walking nearby. Don't be afraid. *Jesu* is mightier than any lion."

As Joshua and his father started to walk up the mountain, Joshua said, "*Wa fisha*."

His father smiled and said, "I know, Joshua. I am hot also, and I am hungry and thirsty."

They saw a mother wearing brightly colored *Sotho* beads. She must have been thirsty too. She was saving *meetse* in a beautiful bottle made from clay near her family *kraal*.

The wind was blowing dry dust around the huts, and the women were trying to sweep it away.

As Joshua passed these villagers,
he could hear bits of stories that told
of joy and healing.

Joshua and his father walked on up the tall mountain. The blue gum trees reached far higher than any neck of a giraffe. Corn stalks were there where the grasses grew wild.

Deep in the tall grass, they stood very still and quietly waved to a young boy.

The boy was standing very close to a giraffe, and they didn't want to frighten him.

Two other boys were sitting outside their family *kraal*. They greeted
Joshua and his father while their
mother cooked *sopo*.

Joshua and his father walked even further up the mountain. They heard a soft voice greet them. *"Thobela le kae?"*

They both yelled back, *"Thobela! Re gona le kae!"* They wanted her to know they were happy to greet her and said they were also well.

She smiled at Joshua and his *tate* as she quickly went back to picking tea leaves.

As she worked, she was singing a
beautiful song.

They only took a few more steps and they could hear more sounds. It was as if an entire choir was singing, and it made Joshua want to dance.

"*Tate*, what is this sound I hear?"

"That, my son, is the greatest sound of all.

It is the praises of the African people reaching up to Heaven where surely all the angels are smiling at the sound of praise from the village."

"But Father, why do the people sing and dance?" asked tired, thirsty Joshua.

"There was a time when there was only sadness in Thabo's village. It was a dark time. The people didn't have food or clean water.

Little children became ill. The African sun seemed to be the enemy. It was too hot. The rains wouldn't come."

"Really, *Tate*? Didn't the people pray?"

"They prayed, but it wasn't until missionaries from another land came and told them about *Jesu* that every person started to feel the hope and love only *Jesu*, the Son of God, could bring.

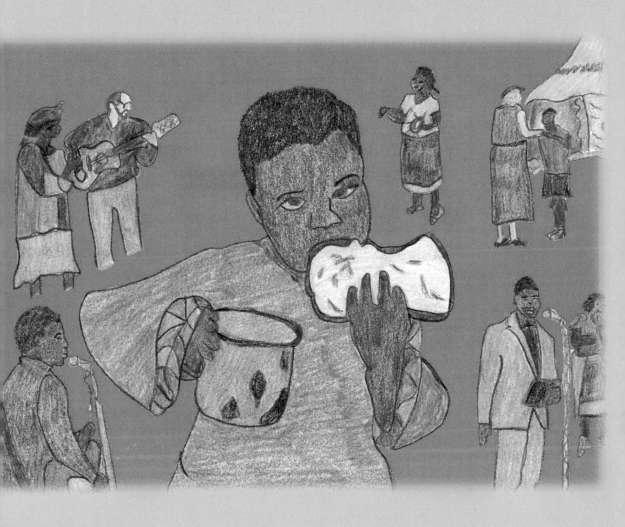

The missionaries brought *dijo*, so the people could eat well and get stronger. They dug wells and gave the people clean water. They prayed in Jesus' name, a name the people had never heard before. In their hearts, the villagers realized that if they believed in Jesus, He would take care of them and keep them safe from harm.

One of the first of the children to love *Jesu* was a young boy named Thabo. He was about twelve years old."

"*Eish*! That's how old I am," said Joshua.

"That is right, my son. Thabo felt

clean and brand new inside when he heard stories of Jesus' love and kindness."

"Then what did he do?"

"Thabo told Jesus he would tell everyone in his village about this great love he had found. A love so powerful that it was able to change darkness into light and to bring joy where there was none.

Thabo did as he promised. He grew tall and strong, learning God's Word. He became a *moruti*, a pastor, at churches he helped build.

Although there were still times of little food and water, it was never again as bad as before. Now, throughout Thabo's village, people who were once sad and sick offered love and praises to Jesus Christ. They knew He had saved them once and He would save them again.

That's why they sing and dance, Joshua. These are their praises. They are thankful for all *Jesu* brought to their village.

Joshua, come. We will go deeper into the village and meet the man called Thabo. He is gathering the people and will tell us about *Jesu*."

"*Tate*, will Jesus be there?" asked Joshua getting excited.

"Oh yes, Joshua. He is already there, and He is always here with us wherever we go."

As they walked deeper into the homelands, they saw much activity throughout the villages. Joshua and his father could hear the rhythm of drums and smell delicious food cooking.

Seeing all of the children made
Joshua want to join in.

Children were playing—

young girls were visiting—

—and women were cooking porridge outside the church.

Laughter could be heard as the children played around one of the mother's cooking *melie* porridge.

Joshua and his father saw three school children eating the yummy porridge as they sat under a tree.

It was close to evening as they finally reached Thabo's village. The prayer meeting had begun. Children, like Joshua, were singing, dancing and praying.

Then it became quiet. Everyone listened to Thabo telling stories of Jesus and how He loves the people.

Joshua and his father felt such love in Thabo's village that they wanted to stay forever, but it was time to bid farewell.

They waved and then called, "*Gabotse!*"

One of the *Sotho* women waved back and yelled, "*Robala, gabotse!* Good-bye and have a good night."

Joshua and his father must return to their own village and tell all they saw and heard of this great King named Jesus.

"*Tate*, I hope we can visit Thabo's village again."

"Me, too, my son."

Thabo's village invites you to come and be loved.

Jesus is waiting.

Note from the Author

I had the pleasure of living with the beautiful people in these villages. They had a brightness about them. My desire to put all I saw to words and pictures has finally come to fruition. I want children globally to know the love of Jesus and to experience His life-changing power, so they can also walk with Him daily.

Activities

- ❖ Have children try to pronounce Northern Pedi words using the glossary and story. Let them rehearse greeting each other.
- ❖ Have children draw some of the items the missionaries brought to share Jesus' love.
- ❖ Cook some corn meal, polenta, in the texture of porridge. Have children try some with butter or milk and sugar.
- ❖ If in a group setting, have children make props and set up a village like Thabo's. Give them parts to play.
  Example: ladies sweeping, cooking, picking tea leaves, men digging dirt to build huts, walking cattle, or men and women singing, dancing or teaching.

Questions

- ❖ What was the Sotho mother with colorful beads saving in her clay bottle? How is that word pronounced?
- ❖ What were the sounds Joshua and his father heard in the villages?
- ❖ Why were the people happy enough to dance?
- ❖ Thabo, at age 12, felt clean and brand new inside. Why?
- ❖ What did young Thabo promise Jesus?
- ❖ Did he keep his promise? How do you know this?

❖ The people prayed but what name had they never heard before the missionaries came?

Salvation Message

Thabo felt clean and brand new inside. How does Jesus make us clean? What makes us unclean inside?

Explain to children how when we do things that are sinful it makes our hearts unclean. The Bible says we can confess our sins and Jesus will clean us on the inside. Sin is doing things our own way and not how God wants us to. But we must ask Jesus to forgive us and ask Him to help us not do what is sinful again.

The Bible also says Jesus loved us way before we were born. He knows we cannot do things His way without His help. Because sin has to be dealt with, He took our punishment for us. We can use our voices to thank Him for all He has done for us.

Ask children if they would like to pray, asking Jesus to forgive them and make them clean and brand new inside like Thabo did.

Jesus gave up His life and made a way for us to be saved—to be made new and clean children of God. Having Jesus as our savior means we accept the gift He gave us, ask Him to forgive us, and thank Him by living our lives for Him.

90976143R00027

Made in the USA
Lexington, KY
16 June 2018